My Best Friend DUC TRAN

Other *Best Friend* Books

My Best Friend, Elena Pappas
    Meeting a Greek-American Family
    by Phyllis Yingling

My Best Friend, Martha Rodriguez
    Meeting a Mexican-American Family
    by Dianne MacMillan and Dorothy Freeman

DIANNE MACMILLAN AND DOROTHY FREEMAN

My Best Friend
DUC TRAN

Meeting a
Vietnamese-American
Family

Pictures By Mary Jane Begin

Julian Messner ⋈ New York
A Division of Simon & Schuster, Inc.

Text copyright © 1987 by Dorothy Freeman and Dianne M. MacMillan
Illustrations Copyright © 1987 by Mary Jane Begin

All rights reserved including the right of reproduction in whole or in part in any
form. Published by Julian Messner, A Division of Simon & Schuster, Inc.,
Simon & Schuster Building, Rockefeller Center, 1230 Avenue of the
Americas, New York, New York 10020

JULIAN MESSNER and colophon are
trademarks of Simon & Schuster, Inc.
10 9 8 7 6 5 4 3 2 1
Manufactured in the United States of America
Library of Congress Cataloguing in Publication Data
MacMillan, Dianne.
My best friend Duc Tran. Meeting a Vietnamese-American
family.

Summary: An American boy's friendship with a
Vietnamese-American boy and his family introduces him to
the holidays, customs, foods, and family events of
their culture.
[1. Vietnamese Americans—Social life and customs—
Fiction. 2. Family life—Fiction. 3. Friendship—
Fiction] I. Freeman, Dorothy Rhodes. II. Title.
PZ7.M2279Mye 1987 [E] 86-21839
ISBN: 0-671-63707-X

305.2 new category · subcultures

Contents

Acknowledgments

The authors wish to thank Dr. Kamchong Luangpraeseut, Supervisor, Indochinese Program, Santa Ana Unified School District; Giao A. Pham, the Vietnamese Community of Orange County, Inc.; Dieu Dinh Le, Editor, *Nguoi Viet Newspaper;* Michael J. Merrifield, ESL/Anthropology Dept., Saddleback College, Mission Viejo, California; and especially Dr. Duong Cao Pham, who was most generous with his professional knowledge and deep understanding of the Vietnamese community.

❧ 1 ❧

Visiting Ph'o' Tran

I met my best friend the first day I moved to California. He rode his bike past my apartment steps, and said "Hi!" Then he circled back around and stopped.

"I'm Duc Huu Tran," he said.

I guess I looked puzzled about his name because Duc said, "I'm Vietnamese."

"Well, I'm Eddie Johnson and I'm from Kansas City." We both laughed and became friends.

We are the only fourth graders in our building. There are lots of older kids, like Duc's sister Diem, who's sixteen, and younger ones like my sister Jill, who's seven.

Duc got me on his soccer team. He's a good player. He said his older brother, Hai, helped him learn. Hai played a lot of soccer when he was a boy in Vietnam. Now Hai is married. He and his wife and little boy, Tuan, live with Duc's family. Tuan's nickname is Cu and he's two years old.

We're hungry after soccer. When we go to Duc's house, his *bà nội* (grandmother) gives us a snack. My favorite is something that looks like a tennis ball covered with

1

sesame seeds. It's crisp on the outside and hollow and sticky on the inside. She calls it *bánh cam*. It tastes sweet, like a doughnut.

Duc's family owns a restaurant. It's called *Pho' Tran*. Everyone in his family except his *bà nội* and Cu work there. Duc rides his bike to the restaurant after school and gets the tables ready for dinner. Sometimes I help him. On each table we put a red tablecloth, a jar full of spoons and chopsticks, and bottles of sauces. We fold red napkins into fancy shapes like birds and put them on the tables.

Duc's mother says that in Vietnam, restaurants don't have tablecloths and napkins, but she likes them because they make the restaurant look beautiful. It was her idea to put mirrors on one wall and red and gold wallpaper on the others.

Duc's mother is the cashier and his father supervises the kitchen. Duc's brother, Hai, and his sister, Diem, wait on customers. Diem also designed the covers of the menus. "Red and gold are the colors of Vietnam," she said as she pointed to the gold dragon on the red cover. When it's time for the restaurant to open for dinner Duc and I go home.

Before we leave, Duc's father says we can choose a treat. I like a drink that he says is green beans and coconut milk. It doesn't look or taste like the green beans I've had at home. The beans taste like chestnuts. It's as good as a milk shake.

I asked Duc if he got tired of working. He looked surprised and said, "My father says our family is our strength and we each have a responsibility to help."

2

❧ 2 ❧

Dinner at the Trans

On Mondays, the restaurant is closed and the Trans have a family dinner at home. When Duc's mother invited me to stay for dinner, my mother said it might be too much trouble for Mrs. Tran.

Duc's mother smiled and said, "There's a Vietnamese saying that if there is a bowl and rice, there is always room for another person."

I sat between Duc and Ky, who had just come from Minnesota to live with the Trans. He's about eighteen.

The first thing at dinner was fish soup. Everyone waited until Bà nội started to eat. We ate with china spoons. Then Diem put a big bowl of rice and a platter filled with pieces of meat and vegetables in the middle of the table. Everyone took some with chopsticks.

I picked up my chopsticks and tried to fit them in my hand. Duc's father watched me and smiled. "Let me show you. Put one in your hand the way you would hold a pencil. Now the other one goes on top of it." He laid one chopstick against my first finger and showed me how to

4

hold the other one between my finger and thumb. "Only the top one moves," he said.

I wiggled the top one back and forth and wondered out loud how I would be able to get any food. Ky filled my plate.

"Don't worry, Eddie," Hai said. "Soon you'll be as good as Cu." I looked at Cu who was eating as fast as his small hands could move.

A pretty woman came into the room and Cu yelled, "Mẹ" (mother) and ran to her. Hai moved over to make room for her at the table. Duc said, "Eddie, this is My-hanh, Hai's wife."

"I'm glad to meet you," she said. "Are you in Duc's class?" I nodded. "Good, then I'll probably see you at school. Tonight I was teaching an adult class at the Vietnamese Community Center. At school I teach ESL."

"ESL is English lessons for Vietnamese kids," Duc explained.

"And for children from Mexico and Iran and the Philippines and even a boy from Holland. My class is a real salad bowl!" My-hanh said.

"Bà nội is learning English, too," Duc said, looking at his grandmother. "She goes to a class at the community center."

"I hope you like this food, Eddie," Duc's mother said.

"I do," I said. "It's really different . . . I mean I don't know what most of it is." Then I felt bad because I thought I'd said the wrong thing.

Diem came to my rescue. "If you think what we have

6

tonight is different, you should see what's in the Vietnamese market."

Duc turned to his father. "Can Eddie go to the shopping center with us on Saturday? And may we go to the pastry shop before we come home?" His father nodded and Duc thanked him.

Family Traditions

After Duc and I helped clear the table, we went into the living room with Duc's father. A bookcase was the largest piece of furniture in the room. Bà nội came in and went up to the bookcase. On the top shelf was a statue, a brass bowl with long sticks of incense, and two red candles. On the second shelf was another brass bowl with incense and a picture of a man. Bà nội lit some incense. It burned with smoke that smelled like perfume.

"That's our family altar," Duc said. "That's my grandfather in the picture. He died in Vietnam. My uncle in San Jose has a bigger altar for all our ancestors because he is the oldest son. Bà nội goes there sometimes, for ceremonies for the ancestors. She used to live with him in San Jose, but the weather was too cold for her."

Hai came into the room with Cu on his shoulders. "The souls of our ancestors protect our family. We pray to them and ask them for help and guidance," he said.

I pointed to the statue and asked who that was.

"That's Buddha."

"Is Buddha a god?" I asked.

"No, he wasn't a god," Hai said. "Buddha was a prince

who lived long ago in India." Hai lifted Cu off his shoulders and put him down on the floor.

Duc's father continued, "Buddha searched for the truths that would make people wiser."

"Did he find them?" I asked.

"Yes, he found what he called the Four Noble Truths that lead to enlightenment." Duc's father looked at the statue of Buddha. "One of the Truths tells us the right way to live."

"What is the right way?" I asked.

"It's complicated. To put it simply, we have to think the right thoughts, speak and believe the right way and find the right way to earn a living."

"That must be hard to do," I said.

"Yes, it is," Duc's father said seriously, "but we keep trying. Everything we do in this life will affect us in our next life."

Bà nội came back into the room. She poured water from a pitcher into small cups on both shelves. Then she put a dish of yellow apples on the altar by the picture and a small vase of flowers by the Buddha.

After she left the room Duc turned on the TV and we watched "The Karate Kid."

"Hai has a seventh degree black belt in martial arts," Duc said proudly. "He teaches it at the police academy."

"Wow!" I said. "I wish I could learn it."

"I'll show you a couple of moves sometime," Hai said.

As I left to go home, Diem said, "Don't forget we're going to the shopping center on Saturday."

"I won't forget!" I answered.

10

❧ 4. ❧

Today Plaza

On Saturday we left early to go to the shopping center. My sister Jill came with us.

"Everybody likes to come on Saturdays to see friends and to talk about Vietnam," Duc said. "My father says this is the largest Vietnamese shopping center in the United States."

The shopping center was several blocks long with hundreds of small stores. We drove under a gigantic red arch guarded by stone lions. Its top was a red tile roof that curved up at the corners. Jill said that it looked like a Chinese temple.

On the front of it was a sign in three languages. I read the English, "Today Plaza."

Duc said, "The other writing is Chinese and Vietnamese. Some of the stores here are owned by Chinese."

Duc's mother said, "I have to go to the grocery store to buy fresh vegetables. Then I have to go to the restaurant and get the cash ready for the day. I'll meet you at the pastry shop at ten-thirty."

"Let's go in the fish market first," said Duc. "There are some things I want to show Eddie." He turned to me. "I hope your nose can stand it."

Duc was right about the way the fish market smelled, but the things I saw were so interesting that I didn't care. There was an octopus with suckers on its arms. I backed away from it and Jill squealed.

"Don't worry, it's dead," Duc said. "Look at these baby ones." He picked up a little one and we all looked at it.

Women were looking in baskets and picking out snails and putting them in bags. In a large tank at the back of the market, crabs were waving their legs at us. In another, catfish were swimming and wiggling their feelers. There were many kinds of fish piled up on ice.

I heard the rock music before we got to the video store. We went in to look around. Diem pointed to posters on the wall and said, "Most of the singers are Chinese."

She introduced us to a boy working behind the counter. "This is Giao. He's in some of my classes at school."

"Are there any Vietnamese rock songs?" I asked.

Giao answered, "Most of the Vietnamese songs are sad. They tell about war and families being separated and remembering Vietnam." He picked out a book and said, "Here's a translation of a Vietnamese song."

A thousand years of Chinese reign,
A hundred years of French domain,
Twenty years of fighting brothers each day.

A mother's fate left for her child,
A mother's fate, a land defiled.

Mothers wait for your kids to come home,
Kids who now so far away roam,
Children of one Mother, one Vietnam.

"That song's really sad," I said. "Do you remember very much about Vietnam?"

Giao didn't say anything.

Duc looked at Diem. "Tell Eddie about the boat," he said.

"Well, I was small, only six or seven when we left Vietnam in a boat."

"I'm seven," said Jill.

"Yes, I was just about your age, Jill," Diem said. "I don't remember a lot except going down inside the boat and being very crowded. I had to sit on Hai's lap. After we sailed out of the bay we were in rough water and the boat rocked back and forth. A lot of people got sick. It was hot and I felt like I could hardly breathe. I was afraid that we were all going to die. It seemed forever until we stopped somewhere. My mother said we went to Thailand and they wouldn't let us land and we had to go on for five days more to Malaysia."

"Did you meet any pirates?" I asked. I had read about the pirates who robbed the people in boats.

"No, we were lucky. I heard about them when we were in the camp in Malaysia."

"My family had to stay in the camp for three months," Duc said.

Giao had been listening and now he added, "The men who owned the boat that I was on were like pirates. They took everything from us. All we saved were our important papers. You were lucky to get out of the camp so soon. We were there for two years."

"I was born in the United States after they got here," Duc said.

The song and the stories were making me feel sad. I was glad when Diem said that we'd better go. "We still have a lot to show Eddie and Jill before we meet my mother in the pastry shop," she said.

We walked through some stores and Diem and Jill stopped to look at some dresses. "Here's what I like," Diem said. "See this long dress with the pants? This is the traditional Vietnamese *aó dài* (dress)." She showed us how each side of the dress was split up to the waist. Then she showed us a beautiful red and gold *aó dài* "That's the Vietnamese wedding dress. After I graduate, I want to study clothing design. I'm going to use ideas from Vietnamese styles," she said.

In a corner of the shop a saleslady was winding strapping tape around a large box until the whole outside was covered. Then she addressed it to someone in Ho Chi Minh City in Vietnam.

"People send material to relatives in Vietnam," said Duc. "They're not allowed to send clothes. Once we sent a raincoat to an uncle but he never got it. Lots of the stuff people send gets stolen."

We walked through a store that Duc said sold Chinese herbs. It smelled like licorice mixed with tobacco. There were drawers all across one wall. Duc said they were filled with herbs for medicine. On a shelf above the drawers was a glass jar filled with dried sea horses.

Duc showed me a little tin filled with an ointment called Tiger Balm. "We rub it on whatever hurts," he said. "It can help a headache or a stomach ache or make you feel better when you have a cold."

"Like the stuff my mom puts on my chest when I have a cold?" I asked.

"Yes," Diem said, "but we also use it when a person has a fever. We put Tiger Balm on his back and shoulders and arms and rub a coin back and forth over it. This brings the blood to the surface and helps cure his fever. It also makes red streaks on his skin."

"Sometimes My-hanh has to explain about Tiger Balm to teachers when Vietnamese children come to school with red marks on their arms," Duc said.

"The grocery store's next," said Diem. We walked farther into the shopping center.

Duc said there was something he wanted to show me. I followed him into the store. He pointed to some boxes and told me to look at what was in them. I saw oval-shaped balls covered with dark gray fuzz.

"Yuck! They look moldy," I said. "What are they?"

"Preserved duck eggs," Duc said.

"Do people really eat those?"

"Sure," Duc said.

Diem looked at her watch. "It's time to meet my mother."

We crossed the street and met Mrs. Tran in the bakery. This place smelled wonderful, like spices and chocolate.

Mrs. Tran said we could each choose a pastry to eat. There were so many pastries that I stood at the counter and couldn't make up my mind which one to have. Jill picked out a croissant filled with cheese.

"I'll have that one," said Duc, pointing to a piece of pastry iced in chocolate. "It has raspberry jelly in the middle."

I took the same kind and looked around for a place to sit. The room was crowded. There were many young men sitting at the tables, drinking small cups of coffee and eating pastries. We found a table for all of us in a corner. Duc moved the stack of Vietnamese newspapers that were on the table.

"People like to come here to read the newspapers and to talk with friends," Diem said.

I took a big bite of the pastry. It was the best thing I ever tasted.

When we finished, Mrs. Tran drove us home because she and Diem had to go back to the restaurant and Duc had to go home and take care of Cu.

❧ 5 ❧

Vietnamese School

A few weeks later I asked Duc if he wanted to go to the movies on Saturday.

"I can't. I have to go to school."

"School? Tomorrow is Saturday!"

Duc said, "I know, but my Vietnamese school is starting again."

"I don't understand. You can already speak Vietnamese. I've heard you talking to Bà nội."

"The school teaches how to read and write Vietnamese. My father wants me to know how. He said he's worried that we'll forget our heritage. Besides, My-hanh teaches the class."

"Do you write with symbols like the Chinese?"

"No. You saw Vietnamese writing in the newspapers and on signs at the shopping center. The letters are the same as English."

I remembered. The letters had lots of marks above and below them. I asked Duc what they meant. He told me that they change the sound and the meaning of the words.

"Why don't you come to class with me? My-hanh won't mind. I'll ask her to make sure."

We walked to class at the Vietnamese Community Center. My-hanh greeted Duc in Vietnamese and then said "hello" to me.

There were maps of Vietnam on the wall. "It's a long, narrow country with a lot of coastline," My-hanh said. She drew an outline of the country and sketched a dragon over it. "Now you'll remember the shape of Vietnam. Sometimes it's called the small dragon, next to China, the big dragon."

The chalkboards were covered with Vietnamese writing and I looked carefully at the marks by the letters. Almost every word had several marks.

The kids sang a song together in Vietnamese. Then they went into reading groups. I could tell from the pictures in the books that some of the stories were ones I knew, like "Little Red Riding Hood."

As we walked home with My-hanh, I asked Duc what his book was about.

"It was a legend about the spirit of the sea fighting with the spirit of the mountains," he said. "That's how our ancestors explained the rainy season in Vietnam."

"Do you have lots of legends?" I asked.

My-hanh answered, "Yes, lots of them. The most common one tells how Vietnam began. A dragon married a fairy named Âu-Cò. They had a hundred sons. Fifty of them went north to the mountains with their mother. The other fifty and their dragon father went south to the sea.

That's why the Vietnamese say they are children of the dragon."

Duc asked, "What do you think of our school, Eddie?"

"I think it's great, but I wouldn't want to go to school on Saturdays. Five days a week are enough!"

My-hanh looked serious. "I know you want to do other things on Saturdays. But in Vietnam, children went to school six days a week. Learning has always been valued by the Vietnamese. Even long ago a whole village would cooperate to send a young man to study at the Imperial Palace. When he passed the court examination the emperor gave him a horse, a red cloak, a piece of land, and a job with the court. Then he made a glorious return to his village to pay homage to his ancestors. People lined the streets cheering for him as he waved a banner signed by the emperor."

"I'd study for a horse and a red cloak," I said.

"Where could you keep a horse?" Duc asked. "I'd rather have a BMX bike and a red racing helmet."

✌ 6 ✌

Karate Class

One afternoon Duc called me on the phone.

"Do you want to go with me when I walk Bà nội to her English lesson? It's at the community center."

"What will we do while she's in class?" I asked.

"The center's next to the junior high so we can shoot baskets on the playground while she has her lesson."

"OK with me," I said.

"Something else . . ." he said. "Could you wear a white shirt? Bà nội says we should dress up to go with her. Wait until you see how she dresses. She says that when you go anywhere in public, you should look your best."

I showed up in my best shirt, but wore a tee shirt underneath for when we shot baskets.

Duc's grandmother was dressed up the way Duc said she would be. She wore a fancy white blouse and black pants. It was hard to talk with her because she doesn't know much English. We walked slowly with her as far as the door of the center and the man in charge invited us to

come in. He greeted her and then spoke into a micro-
phone to introduce us. I bowed my head when I saw Duc
do it. Then we left and went to shoot baskets.

When we came back to the center we had to wait for Bà
nội. Duc and I walked by one of the classrooms. We heard
a loud "hah!"

"That's the karate class. Let's watch," said Duc.

We looked at some young men dressed in white baggy
pants and shirts. They were practicing a karate kick in
slow motion. As they kicked they shouted "hah!"

"That's the back kick," said Duc. "Hai taught me how
to do it. I'll show you." Duc bowed slowly and turned so
his back was toward me. Then he lifted his knee and
looked over his shoulder. In the next second he kicked
toward me and shouted, "hah!"

I tried to do the kick the same way, but lost my balance
and fell on my face.

Duc laughed. "That's OK, Eddie. Balance is one of the
hardest things to learn."

I made up my mind I really wanted to learn karate. I
liked the way the young men moved.

We walked Bà nội home and she said, "Thank you," in
English.

One evening when Hai was home Duc and I told him
about seeing the class in martial arts. Hai told us that
martial arts were a part of a boy's training in Vietnam. He
said he learned when he was fourteen. When Ky came
home he and Hai demonstrated some moves in slow

motion. They told me they were sure I'd be able to learn.

I wondered how Ky came to live with the Trans. I got brave and asked, "Are you a relative?"

"No, an honorary member of the family."

Hai explained, "Our families knew each other in Vietnam. His family is still there. Ky left Vietnam a few months ago and was sent to Minnesota, but it was too cold for him there."

Ky added, "I never saw snow before Minnesota. I was glad to come here."

Hai said, "When you're used to tropical heat it's hard to be in cold, winter weather."

"Do you like living here?" I asked.

"Yes, but I miss my family. I'm afraid I'll never see them again."

Duc said, "He's working in our restaurant and going to school."

"I'm studying how to assemble circuit boards," Ky said.

❧ 7 ❧

A Special Lunch

On my birthday my mom lets me choose the kind of cake I want. She usually bakes it. I told her about the fancy cakes I saw at the pastry shop. I asked her if we could get one there. She said we could.

"How would you like to have lunch at the Tran's restaurant before we buy your cake?" She didn't have to ask twice.

The Tran's restaurant is about three blocks north of the shopping center. My mom was surprised at how fancy the restaurant was. She looked at the red and gold wallpaper and the mirrors on the wall. She especially liked the light fixtures and told me the shiny ornaments were crystals.

Mr. and Mrs. Tran were there and so were Ky and Diem. They were very glad to see us. I asked Mrs. Tran what we should order. "I want my mom to know how good Vietnamese food is."

"Do you want me to select some dishes?" she asked.

"Yes! I'd like that," my mom agreed.

Mr. Tran came out from the kitchen. "Vietnamese

cooking is special. We've used ideas from two of the best kinds of cooking in the world."

"The Chinese?" my mother asked.

"That and the French," Mr. Tran said.

Diem brought four platters of food, one at a time. Mrs. Tran gave us each a bowl of yellow liquid. *"Nu'ó'c mắm,"* she said. "It's a fish sauce. You dip your food in it."

I remembered tasting *nu'ó'c mắm* at the Tran's house.

When we were finished, Mrs. Tran asked my mom, "What did you like best?"

"Everything was delicious, but I especially liked the beef with lemon sauce. Would you tell me how to make it?"

Diem said she'd write down the recipe when she had time. She also told us about the Vietnamese book store that had lots of cookbooks, some in English.

"Shall we go to the book store?" my mom asked after lunch. It was just a few stores from the restaurant. The book store had hundreds of books in Vietnamese.

My mom said, "I'm surprised there are so many translations of American and English classics! Here's Shakespeare and here's Moby Dick!" Then she noticed a large section of poetry books. My mom loves poetry.

The salesman came over and spoke to us. "We Vietnamese always like to think of ourselves as poets. Before we had a written language, we had poetry." My mom bought a poetry book and a cookbook that were both translated into English. I bought a comic book that was written in both languages.

We drove to the pastry shop. I picked out a cake that had chocolate inside and whipped cream and nuts and cherries on the outside.

"This is just like a French bakery," my mom said.

"It is a French bakery, madam," the woman said as she put the cake in a box. "Their pastry was one of the good things the French gave us," she added.

When we were outside I told my mom how the French had occupied Vietnam for over a hundred years. I remembered that from Giao's song.

❧ 8 ❧

The Vietnamese Year

On Sunday afternoon Duc and Diem and Ky came to have birthday cake with us. Ky had never seen a birthday cake and he was surprised by the candles. I explained that I made a wish and blew them out.

"What do you do to celebrate birthdays?" I asked.

"We don't celebrate them," Ky said.

That puzzled me. "How do you know how old you are?" I asked.

"Oh, we know our birth date, but we have our first birthday on *Tết* and every year after that we're a year older on *Tết*." Diem said.

"What's *Tết*?"

Diem said, "*Tết* is the beginning of the lunar new year. The Vietnamese calendar has months the length of the cycle of the moon. *Tết* is a three-day celebration for the new year. Everyone gets a year older on *Tết*. We don't pay as much attention to a person's birthday as we do to the anniversary of his death day."

"That sounds strange," I said.

"It really isn't," Diem continued. "It's an important holiday called *ngày giỗ*, a day for remembering. We celebrate my grandfather's *ngày giỗ*. My uncle is responsible for five generations of ancestors."

"Wow! That's a lot of relatives," I said.

"It's the duty of the oldest son to carry out the ceremonies for the family," Diem said. "On my grandfather's anniversary all our relatives and close friends are invited. Each guest brings an offering, like tea or wine. We pray to my grandfather's spirit and put a plate of food on the altar for him. Then we have a special dinner. We talk about all the good things he did. It's really a happy time."

"You and I sure have some different ways," I said.

"Yes, like how you write your name," Ky said. "It's hard for me to remember."

Duc said, "Vietnamese write and say their last name first. In Vietnam my name is said this way: Tran Huu Duc. The family name isn't very important because there aren't very many Vietnamese family names. Almost everyone is called Nguyen, like Ky, or Tran, like us. Our first names are the most important and they have meanings."

"That is different," I said. "What does your name mean?"

Duc looked embarrassed and then said, "It means 'to have virtue.' Cu's real name, Tuan, means 'famous.' Diem means 'beautiful.' "

"Something else that's different is that women usually keep their own family names when they marry," Diem said.

"But I call your mother Mrs. Tran."

"That's OK, she understands American ways."

"Something that is the same," Duc said, "is that we all like this cake!"

❧ 9 ❧

Holiday Preparations

One afternoon during the last week of January, I stopped by Duc's apartment to see if he was ready to go to soccer practice. His grandmother opened the door. She was dressed in her fancy blouse and black pants.

"Is Bà nội going to the community center?" I asked.

"No, Hai is taking her to the airport. She's going to San Jose to celebrate *Tết* with my uncle."

Bà nội spoke to Duc in Vietnamese and then pointed to me. "She says to tell you that the celebration in Vietnam was much bigger than it is here. She's sad that we can't celebrate here like she used to in Vietnam. She says she's thinking of all the people left behind."

"Why doesn't she celebrate here with your family?"

"Remember, I told you that the family's main altar is in my uncle's house? She will celebrate there."

"What do you do for *Tết*?"

Duc answered, "We have special food and do a lot of visiting with friends. It's an honor to be asked to be the first *Tết* visitor. That person is the one who will bring good luck to the family for the year."

"What if he doesn't bring good luck?"

"Then he's responsible for the bad luck, too," Duc said. "The part I like best is getting money for toys and candy. Our family and the visitors give us money in red envelopes call *phong bao*. Wait a minute. I'll show you one."

In a moment he gave me a red envelope about the size of my hand. It had a gold dragon printed on it. "Red is the color for *Tết*, like red and green are Christmas colors," he said. "Right before midnight my father offers food to our ancestors and invites them to join us. At midnight we light firecrackers and beat on drums. Then my father welcomes in the new year."

"What about the special food you talked about?"

Duc said, "My mother makes *bańh chu'ng* (rice cakes). They are made of sticky rice and pork and soy beans. We wrap some of them in red cellophane to give to friends who visit."

"On Sunday we're going to the big *Tết* celebration in the park. It's like a carnival with games and dances and food. It celebrates the new year. Each year is named for an animal and this is the year of the cat. I'll ask my father if you can come with us."

"I hope he says I can!"

"I'm sure he will. He told me that you're welcome in our family."

❧ 10 ❧

Celebrating Tết

Since I met the Trans I've seen so many new things. *Tết* at the park was the best. There were booths where you could win prizes. Hai won a big teddy bear for Cu by hitting cans and knocking them over.

We saw Duc's mother sitting on the grass. She was with some friends and she motioned for us to come there. She handed each of us a *bánh bao*. It was barbecued beef on a bamboo stick.

"Thanks," I said. Then I tasted it. "This is super!"

Mrs. Tran said, "Diem, here's some money for you and Eddie and Duc to buy some other food. Be sure Eddie tries the spring rolls."

"Hey, look over there," Duc said. "They're starting the new year's play."

The play was in Vietnamese, so I didn't understand what they were saying. I knew it was funny because all the people watching were laughing.

"The one in the purple robe is the kitchen god," Diem explained. "The other one, in the red robe, is the king of the heavens. The kitchen god is telling the king all the

things that have happened this past year. Most of them are made up and are pretty silly." As we watched, the kitchen god pointed to people in the audience and the crowd laughed. "He's telling stories on some people," she said. "I have to go get ready now. I'll see you later."

She left and I asked Duc where she was going.

"She's going to dance," he said. "She's in the group that does Vietnamese dances. You'll see."

Mrs. Tran joined us and said, "Tết is a time to think about the old year and hope for the new one, just like your New Year's Day. In Vietnam it was a time to pay debts, return borrowed things, forgive one another and shop to buy new clothes and gifts. So it's like Christmas, New Year's Day, and birthdays combined."

When the play was over we walked past a booth selling stereos, video recorders, and tape players. Ky liked that. He told us that he knew how to assemble the circuit boards for some of them.

On the far side of the park there was a display of large color photographs and maps of Vietnam. "Here is where we lived," Mr. Tran said, pointing to a city on the map.

Duc looked at a picture of a temple. "I know that one, it's the Temple of Remembrance in Ho Chi Minh City. My-hanh had a picture of it in our class."

"The city was called Saigon," said Mr. Tran softly. He stood in front of the picture for a long time.

"The dancing's next," Duc said. "Now you'll see Diem."

When I saw her with the dancers I thought she looked

like a movie star. She was dressed in a white *aó dài* like the one she had shown Jill. She and the other dancers had fans with lots of colors on them. When I told my mother about it later, I said that the fans looked like birds flying.

Duc told me that the dancers belong to a club that wants to keep the old traditions alive. "Diem's the best dancer," he said. "She's been dancing since she was ten."

Duc and I wandered around some more and bought Cu a red balloon. We stayed at the *Tết* celebration until dark. As we left I said, "Thanks, today was really great."

"I'm glad we're friends," Duc said.

"Me, too," I said. "You're my best friend, Duc Huu Tran!"

38

Some Books about Vietnam

Buell, Hal. *Viet Nam, Land of Many Dragons.* New York: Dodd, Mead & Company, 1968.

Dareff, Hal. *The Story of Vietnam.* New York: Parents Magazine Press, 1971.

Newman, Bernard. *Let's Visit Vietnam.* Bridgeport, Connecticut: Burke Publishing Company, Ltd., 1983.

Stanek, Muriel. *We Came from Vietnam.* Niles, Illinois: Albert Whitman & Company, 1985.

Tran, Van Dien. *Folktales for Children.* Skokie, Illinois: National Textbook Company, 1982.

Vuong, Lynette. *The Brocaded Slipper and Other Vietnamese Tales.* Reading, Massachusetts: Addison-Wesley, 1982.

About the Authors

Dianne MacMillan grew up in St. Louis, Missouri, and graduated from Miami University in Ohio with a Bachelor of Science Degree in Education. She taught school for many years but now spends her time writing. Her stories have appeared in, *Highlights for Children, Jack and Jill,* and *Cobblestone,* and she is the co-author of *My Best Friend, Martha Rodriguez.* She lives in Anaheim, California with her husband and three children.

Dorothy Rhodes Freeman is an educator and author of twenty-one books, including *Someone for Maria,* and *A Home for Memo.* She is also the co-author of *My Best Friend, Martha Rodriguez.* Mrs. Freeman currently writes bilingual education projects and monitors and evaluates the results. Writing is both her vocation and hobby. She has two grown children and lives with her husband in Placentia, California.

JERABEK ELEMENTARY SCHOOL
10050 AVENIDA MAGNIFICA
SAN DIEGO, CA 92131